RED DEER
COLLEGE
PRESS

56 Avenue & 32 Street
Box 5005, Red Deer, Alberta
Canada T4N 5H5

**We are pleased to enclose
a complimentary review copy of**

Title: The Prowler

Author: Kristjana Gunnars

Publication Date: April 1989

Binding: Hardcover/jacketed trade paper

Price: $19.95 hardcover/$9.95 trade paper

We would appreciate two copies
of your review or notification
of your broadcast review schedule.

For more information contact:
Dennis Johnson, Managing Editor
(403) 342-3402 Fax (403) 340-8940

D0793075

Kristjana Gunnars

The Prowler

Kristjana Gunnars

The Prowler
a novel

Red Deer College Press

The Publishers
Red Deer College Press
56 Avenue and 32 Street, Box 5005
Red Deer, Alberta, Canada T4N 5H5

Credits
Designed by Peter Bartl/word and image
Typesetting by Pièce de Résistance Ltée.
Printed and bound in Canada by
First Western Printing Ltd.

Acknowledgements
The publishers gratefully acknowledge the financial
contribution of the Alberta Foundation for the Literary
Arts, Alberta Culture and Multiculturalism, the Canada
Council, Red Deer College, and Radio 7 CKRD.

Canadian Cataloguing in Publication Data

Gunnars, Kristjana, 1948-
The Prowler
ISBN 0-88995-043-1 (bound)
ISBN 0-88995-042-3 (pbk.)
I. Title
PS8563. U574P7 1989 C813'.54 C89-091040-5
PR9199.3G86P7 1989

for Gunnar, my father

The story of my life doesn't exist. Does not exist. There's never any center to it. No path, no line. There are great spaces where you pretend there used to be someone, but it's not true, there was no one.

– Marguerite Duras, *The Lover*

1

Perhaps it is not a good book, he said, James Joyce said, *but it is the only book I am able to write.* It is not a book I would ever read from. I would never again stand in front of people, reading my own words, pretending I have something to say, humiliated. It is not writing. Not poetry, not prose. I am not a writer. Yet it is, in my throat, stomach, arms. This book that I am not able to write. There are words that insist in silence. Words that betray me. He does not want me to write this book. The words make me sleep. They keep me awake.

2

We were standing and staring at each other. It was an unexpected meeting. Perhaps because of that no one was able to speak. I was noticing a certain aura, an extraordinary substance without physical properties. Something I had detected before, but I was not sure where.

There are some moments that seem to be live ones. It is not that other moments are dead, but I am not sure what they are. Moments that bring in a host of other moments, those are the live ones.

I was thinking something over.

There must have been something that determined the sudden configuration of thoughts. A shattering experience, perhaps. A card game that did not add up. A game where there were no winners. I was not sure that there would ever be any winners.

3

It is a relief not to be writing a story. Not to be imprisoned by character and setting. By plot, development, nineteenth century mannerisms. A relief not to be writing a poem, scanning lines, insisting on imagery, handicapped by tone. A relief just to be writing.

4

I do not want to be clever. To make myself laugh. I do not feel clever. If I laugh at myself, it is because I have nothing to say and I am full of love. Because nothing I can say says anything. There will be mere words.

It is because I am full of love that my words have no meaning.

5

It is a book marked by its ordinariness. That knows there can be nothing extraordinary in a life, in a language.

6

Yet the story intrudes. Where did it begin? How far back can you take cause and effect until your story starts? I could go back to the day of my birth, but that is too far. Or back to the day my father came out of the airplane that took him far away. He brought in his suitcase Toblerone chocolates and stories of gypsies.

But my father was always going far away in airplanes and bringing home Toblerone chocolates. He did not tell stories of gypsies. My sister and I made up the stories. The gypsies were out on the Hungarian plains, and our father went to see them. He was in love with a gypsy. He stole our mother and brought her back, for she was a gypsy as well.

7

We had visits from Dr Patel. Dr Patel was a short East Indian man with a dark complexion, something like cocoa. He smiled a great deal. When he came to dinner, my mother did not know what to cook. Dr Patel did not eat meat, and there were no vegetables in our country.

My sister and I sat in anticipation at the table and worried about Dr Patel. He would die of starvation. But he was laughing.

Dr Patel did not speak our language, and my sister and I did not speak English. But if he asked about the vegetables, what do you then eat? we would say: we are the white Inuit. We eat fish. And in summers we graze like sheep among the mountain grasses.

8

It is true we grazed like sheep in the mountains. I cannot deny it. In the spring it was a preoccupation to hunt for those sour dark green leaves that grew among the grasses in the hills. The ones we called sourdogs. And I ate daisies, carefully picking out the yellow disks. On the shore we gathered wild rhubarb, nibbling as we went.

During the war it was said people scraped up those unappetizing strings of seaweed that lay on the rocks by the water. I thought about it.

In the fall everyone took to the hills, sometimes to the remote interior, to pick berries. It was important. Families took time from work and spent days filling buckets with currant berries and blueberries.

On rare occasions a lemon would appear in our house. It would have come in the cargo of some fishing boat that stopped in Bremerhaven or Hull. I was like a prospector eyeing gold. I was stuck to the lemon, thirstily devouring the juice, the meat, the rind, everything but the seeds.

9

I do not think this is the story of a starving nation. During the Cuban crisis and the Korean war, the decade after World War II, we did have cod roe and cod liver, whale meat and sheep heads. On holidays and Sundays we always had legs of lamb.

My sister was so thin her bones stuck out of her sweater. She had sores on her hands. It was some form of malnutrition. I thought the boats should bring more vegetables, surely.

At school we received CARE packages from the United States. Small boxes were distributed to each child sitting patiently at his desk while the woman went from one to the other. I opened my box. It contained some tiny used toys donated by some American family. I rummaged among these useless objects, looking for a lemon.

10

Since there was no fruit, and there were no vegetables, there were no trees either. If there were trees once on these mountains, they had all been cut away. There was a great campaign to plant trees. At bus stops, in shop windows, on postage stamps, there was the slogan: *Let us clothe the land.*

We had very few clothes. I was always cold, and when it rained I was always wet. It was a thought so selfish I hardly dared think it: *I* need clothes. My body needs clothes.

At night I fell asleep shivering. It often took many hours to warm up, curled in a ball under the quilt, and finally sleep came to the exhausted, still shivering.

It was not a country where children spoke to the adults. Only the adults spoke to the children. I could not say: father, I am cold and need more clothes.

Later, much later, when I had been in America for a long time, my timidity finally collapsed. I had money in my wallet. I went into one of the thousands of stores filled to the brim with clothes and began to buy them. I bought clothes for all kinds of weather and shoes for all kinds of ground. Especially for rain. Never again would I be wet and cold. I bought a carload full of clothes and felt like a criminal.

11

Somewhere in all this, the story begins. It is not *my* story. If there is a God, it is God's story.

12

Sometimes I saw my mother would stop her weaving and look out the window. Perhaps she was remembering a better place than this.

There would be snowflakes coming down.

If it had been a country where children spoke to adults, I would have said: you are lucky that family of yours came up from the Hungarian plains to the Danish peninsula. And you are lucky that my father, the white Inuit, found you there and brought you to this island where there are many seals and where occasionally a polar bear drifts over on the Greenland ice.

I knew this was true because we had a radio. On the radio the woman said there was a revolution in Hungary, and then there was an invasion. Russian tanks went into Budapest.

13

On the bus I met the beautiful black-haired young woman who once lived in my village. She had gone to America, where there were more flowers and trees than could be counted. I said to her: why on earth are you here? It is raining and cold. She told me the president, President Kennedy, ordered everybody to go home where they came from. Why? I asked. There is a missile crisis in Cuba, you fool, she said. Is there no radio in your house?

I did not know what a missile crisis was, but I knew what a cold war was.

On the street my girlfriend and I met two American soldiers. We must have been fourteen. They wanted us to come into the hotel and smoke cigarettes. That is how I knew about the cold war.

Later I was told the American soldiers had been cordoned off at the American Base. There was a fence around the Base, and the men were not allowed to go out. Even then it was not time to speak, but I would have said: that is the right thing to do. Because American soldiers are interested in children.

14

In the following decade I came to know those American soldiers, as people, in their own country. Some were my friends. They played music, sang ballads, wrote poetry like other people. I knew them before they went to war, naive and happy, and after they came back from war, not so naive and much more cruel. It was no longer a cold war. It was the time when the television showed many pictures of maimed Asian children.

15

Who are the people looking over my shoulder, writing stories in my name? Is it my great-great-grandfather from the remote north of Thingeyjarsýsla, who had so much to do with the liberation of my father's people from the clutches of my mother's people? Or is it my great-grandfather from the Danish island of Fyn, who gambled away his entire estate? If that man ever wrote a will, there could have been nothing in it.

16

In my father's country I was known as the dog-day girl, a monarchist, a Dane. Other kids shouted after me: King-rag! Bean!

In my mother's country other kids circled me haughtily on their bicycles. They whispered among each other on the street corners that I was a white Inuit, a shark-eater. The Icelander.

My sister did not care for this injustice. She went on a hunger strike against God.

17

Perhaps the person telling these stories is a little older. The distinctly lonely girl in Rungsted, Denmark, who had been made to understand that Isak Dinesen lived next door. Perhaps it is someone older still. The girl who lived in the Mosfellssveit hills in Iceland, who was told repeatedly that Halldór Laxness lived on the next farm. That white house you see from your window.

Or it is someone even older, in a small town near the Oregon coast. The one who was made aware that Bernard Malamud lived in her house. He wrote *The Fixer* in your room.

It is someone in the trail of ghosts.

18

The person writing these words is probably the one who sits beside hospital beds, not knowing what to say. It is an occupation I began at the age of twelve. I sat by my sister, who was older than I. She lay bone-thin on the bed, her cheekbones protruding, her eyes large. Why do you not want to eat? I asked her. People who refuse to eat die. She answered me. I just don't want to be who I am, she said.

19

It is the only consistency in the fragments of what I no longer remember. There have been so many voices, but the one that sits beside hospital beds is always the same. It is no voice at all. It has nothing to say.

Perhaps, I thought, on my way in the train from Rungsted to Copenhagen, walking along the broad boulevard lined with trees, through the gates of the large hospital, perhaps, even though I say nothing, just being there is enough. My sister was putting on weight because they were forcing her to eat. I sat beside her revengefully grim face. No doubt she is planning a revolution, I thought. She is planning to punish everyone for being who she is.

There are things we know long before we know them.

Some of us receive gifts that seem to be open doorways out of dilemmas. It is a kind of CARE package from fate. I was one of the fortunate ones, for at the age of thirteen or fourteen my blond hair turned brown. When that happened everyone thought I was Russian because that is what I looked like. I was called the little Russian girl and was content with that.

20

I helped spread the rumor once it was begun. I studied Pasternak, Yevtushenko, Pushkin. To prove the point I showed my friends the Russian books in my father's bookshelf, the ones with the strange inverted alphabet. If they were incredulous I asked my father to say some words in Russian, which he did. It was my good fortune that Russian was one of my father's languages.

21

Anything that came from far away was good. Life elsewhere was magical. The further away it was, the more magical.

I sometimes stood in front of the mirror in the hall, rehearsing pinched eyes and Japanese words. Life is not enough, I insinuated to the mirror. It has to be magic.

22

In the rubbish of one of my annual CARE packages from the United States, distributed to us at school, I discovered two brown-haired rubber dolls, each the size of my thumb. Around these dolls I built an entire world that was to last for the rest of my childhood. They acquired a house with furniture, names, a language, invisible friends, things to do.

That dollhouse was located in the loft, which could only be reached through a hole in the ceiling, on a makeshift ladder hung by nails to the wall. No one else ever went up there. If all the hours I spent in the loft, under the skylight window in the roof, were counted, they would constitute at least a year of a person's life.

23
But it is not these things I love.

It is a world that never was. Perhaps I love the aspiration. The fantasy. Perhaps it is only the desire that I love.

24
For a story it is enough to find the beginning. Because the end is contained in the beginning. The fulfillment is contained in the desire.

The answer is also contained in the question.

I imagine a story that has no direction. That is like a seed. Once planted, the seed goes nowhere. It stays in one place, yet it grows in itself. It blossoms from inside, imperceptibly. If it is a vegetable, it nourishes.

25
I have read treatises on male writing. The male line. The masculine story. That men have to be going somewhere. Men are always shooting something somewhere. And that women do not. That women can

grow all things in one place. That the female story is an unfolding of layers.

I do not know if this is true. It is incidental.

26

There were vegetable plots tended by school-children. Every child had an assigned garden patch and was expected to work in it for three or four hours every day. There was a slogan on the radio, in the papers, on the walls of banks and pharmacies: *Work in the school gardens.*

It was a way of bringing vegetables to an undernourished nation.

I had a patch on the south side of our village, just above the shore. Every day I hoed, raked, weeded or planted in it. There were radishes, cabbages, turnips, potatoes. I planted them and watched them grow, cleaning the patch daily.

I did not like this work. It was tedious. The hours were long. I was tired and those dumb plants bored me. But in the end I could begin to bring them home. The dirty radishes I carried home to my mother's kitchen were something very small I had to give after all.

Perhaps there was some pride contained in this gift. In a country where children were not taught to be proud, and where girls lived under the national suspicion of being potential *American-soldier-whores*, there was some pride in this work. But it made me hate gardening.

27

But is this why, much later in life, I could never take an American lover? Because with a Korean or a Greek or a Hungarian, you can be with a dark and handsome man from a magical place, a man who is difficult, obscure, who plays games with your emotions. But with these understanding Americans, it is understood you are a whore and you do it for money?

28

It is a relief to be under no obligation. Not to have to balance the books. Not to count the cash at the end of the day. Not to count the pages as they accumulate. Not to think about a climax or a denouement or an introduction. Instead just to watch the egg hatch. It is there and I know it will hatch.

I have often thought, if God were a writer He would write such a curious story. It would take you into many false corners. It would be a maze, and you would not understand it. Repeatedly you would have to backtrack, retrace your steps, acknowledge defeat. Then in the end there would be an ironic twist.

You would not see the irony right away. But it would slowly dawn on you. It would be pure irony.

29

I waited for the bus on the last day of school. The National Exams were over. We had received our report cards and all been cleared to go into the world. I was waiting in an empty classroom. The late afternoon sun had gone to the other side of the old schoolhouse. From the window I could see the mountains I hiked over every day with my books and notepaper. I observed how cracked the walls of the building were, how run-down, worn. Paint had peeled off in large patches. The desks were riddled with knife markings.

Magnús, the language teacher, came into the room. I looked up. Well, he said, school is over. It took me another twenty-two years to understand that simple statement.

30

Reading *Morgunbladid*, the Icelandic daily, I saw the population of the island was being reassured. The American Base, it said, is not a nuclear base. Some months later in Canada I happened upon an American military map. Iceland, it showed, *is* a nuclear base.

Is there any reason to believe that the sense we make of things is good sense?

Some Icelandic novels make no sense. They are not meant to make sense. They go nowhere, refuse to grasp reality, say there is no reality. Potentially there is no reality. My father's people have always known that potentially they do not exist.

31

My first story was written at the age of sixteen. It was written out of longing, in a town near the Oregon coast and in that room where *The Fixer* was written. Every night before sleep I wrote a section in my story, in poor English, about a girl who wanted to go home. Somehow she still knew where home was.

It must have been the shore in the fjord below our house. Every stone there was familiar to me. I knew the barnacles and shells and seaweed better than I knew any other place. Our playground was a stranded tanker, rusty throughout from lying on its side on the sand in the shallow water. Sometimes we forgot ourselves on the old wreck and the tide rose, isolating us part way out in the fjord. We could not get back to the shore.

32

I went with my father to the black desert sands on the southern coast of the island. They were searching for the submerged wreck of a Spanish ship that had carried gold. The men had metal detectors, and they spread themselves out in all directions, waiting for the signal of gold underground.

I walked out on a sandspit. It was an overcast day. The sand was black, the sea was black, the sky was almost black. As I walked, seals emerged from the water. They stuck their heads out of the sea and followed me as I went. I walked so far and so long that the tide rose behind me, closing access to the mainland. I was out on an island of sand that was preparing to go under.

There was a small shack in that desert. Though it was falling apart in the constant wind, there was still a door to it that could be opened. I went inside. On the shelves were rusty cans of sugar, coffee, flour. For travellers who were lost or stranded.

33

Sometimes there is no door to go through. Schoolchildren were taught by their masters: when that happens it is necessary to compose poems. When you have composed poems long enough, a door will be granted.

34

I remember the eyes of the seals were distinctly sorrowful.

Because I am full of love, I am full of sorrow.

35

If the winter was not too severe, the horses were allowed to wander freely in the mountains. Sometimes in the mornings I woke and saw a stray horse looking in at me though the window. There were grumpy puffing sounds and impatient lip noises.

On occasion I was allowed to sleep out on the heath. Those times I woke at dawn and found usually one or two sheep who had ventured close staring at me. When I moved they scuffled away as if whispering to each other.

36

Conflicting emotions are silencing.

It was not called a hospital, but a health-preservation-center. A red stone building with a tower, which was only accessible by crossing a wide bridge that led to the entrance. Under the bridge lay a chasm of stones. The center was built to eradicate tuberculosis, leprosy, scurvy, polio. In that country those diseases were the national inheritance. They molded the people, their thoughts, their aspirations.

It was my sister's first hospital. Next to the public swimming pool in Reykjavík, where those without baths at home came for their daily shower. I found my way there without difficulty, even as a small girl. I found my sister's bed and could not understand why she was in it. I would have asked her: what on earth are you doing here? but knew there must be a reason.

My mother finally lost her cool. We scrape around in this mud for hours whenever a bit of summer appears to grow a few turnips. We wait for weeks until the herring and cod and haddock come by here so they can be fished out. We pay the price of a house for a few imported Danish apples. Children go about with bleeding gums and adults watch their bones go crooked. And you, she said to my sister, you refuse to eat!

37

My turn came to go to the center when I was nine. I went there in mortification, alone. The doctor's name was Hannes. He ushered me into the small examining room, sat down, looked at me and said: well? In silence I began to peel off my older sister's hand-me-down clothing. Jacket, mittens, sweater, undershirt. I stood in the middle of his room naked to the waist and extended my arms for him to see. There was nothing to say. He could see for himself. My skin. Something had happened to all of my skin.

Hannes examined me, then helped me put my sweater back on and patted the top of my head sadly. If you live in the Middle East, he said, you can maybe go to the Red Sea and wash in it. That will no doubt cure you. But for us way up here in the North there is no hope.

38

I became aware that for us in the North dreams never did come true. They just remained dreams. I will never be Japanese. My mother will never be a Hungarian gypsy. My father will never be Russian. I began to understand my sister.

Where there is no hope, the dream is all. The end is contained in the aspiration. Dreams are the closed mussels lying among the stones in the fjord. The shells are clamped tightly around a small bit of life.

39

This was the country where people died of starvation. For eleven hundred years sheep collapsed in the mountain passes, horses fell dead in the ash-covered pastures, fishermen were too tired to drag nets out of the sea. Children faded away in the sod huts from malnutrition. Old men ate their skin jackets.

Yet the shores were filled with mussels. All along the water, the black and blue closed shells lay by the thousands. People refused to eat the mussels.

40

I did not like the American serviceman who sometimes came to our house. His name was Chuck. I do not care for the memory. It is a nothing memory. A non-memory.

Chuck knew something about drilling bore-holes, so he visited my father. It was a country that needed geothermal energy so there could be industry and growth. Chuck always brought presents. He came to our house with a television, a radio, toys, Disney-land tinsel things, candy in shiny wrappers. I was instructed to thank him for the gifts. I did so. Then I took them outside and secretly put them in the garbage can.

Even at that time I knew you must not keep that which does not belong to you. There are some people who deserve unearned prizes, but those people are all far away.

41

Your sister has done so well in school before you, Ármann the high school principal said to me in his office, and you have shown such promise that we have decided to let you skip a grade. Also you already speak Danish.

He was grinning warmly. I understood he had just given me the right to speak. So I said bluntly:

if I'm so smart, then the question I have must be legitimate. Go ahead, he invited me. I said: in the Bible there are a lot of lepers. But why is this the only place in Northern Europe where there are lepers?

Because this, Ármann explained, pointing to the ground, is where other countries dumped their lepers. They did not think the people on this remote island counted.

What other countries? I asked. Why? But he did not answer me. He just stood in one spot, looking at me with a warm grin on his face. That is the grin I imagine he still had on his face when he died.

42

Our house was in the west end, and the school stood in the east end. The road between took me along the shoreline of the fjord south of town. The water lay blank between the two peninsulas, shining with the silver of the sky. In the bottom of the fjord there was a fenced-off area containing a large white building that had been there for decades. Long before the town was built, this building was there. It was the leprosy sanatorium. Twice a day I walked by it, refusing to look.

43

Somewhere else in town there was a tuber-culosis sanatorium. People were taken to these places and imprisoned for life.

Every year they put a band-aid on our bony chests. Every year they took the band-aid off a week later and made notes in big books. We lined up like prisoners awaiting sentence. We called it terror day. The nurse assured us: this is nothing special. It is done all over the world.

44

Also you already speak Danish. He meant I could begin to answer my own questions now.

I had other questions. Such as, why are there no Icelandic dances?

Why has there been such a long history of starvation?

45

Later I read the history of Iceland's involve-ment in World War II. One morning during the war, I read, people woke up to find they were occupied by the British. This was to preempt the possible arrival of the Germans. British soldiers flooded the streets. The radio spoke English. Wartime barracks were constructed on the outskirts of town.

Then just as suddenly the British were gone, and people woke up to find they were occupied by the Americans. Cartoons in the papers showed how the women were the first to know about this change. All of a sudden their British sweethearts were American. Ugly novels appeared, written by Icelandic men, about women who were traitors.

46

Since then, every year Icelandic communists have marched the fifty kilometers from Reykjavík to the American Base in Keflavík. Everywhere there were slogans: *Away with the Base!*

My great-aunt Sirrí was the daughter of a statesman whose face is on the fifty crown note. When I visited the old woman, she always gave me oranges from the Base. Why are they marching? she asked, her skinny hands shaking as she peeled me the precious orange. The Americans have done us nothing but good, she said.

Many years later, in America, there was a broadcast on the nuclear capacity of the United States. I happened to see this, and there was a map of the Nordic countries, Iceland and Greenland. In case of a world war, the announcer said, of course the first target of attack will be Iceland. That will be to preempt any possible retaliation by the Americans from their strategic North Atlantic position.

If the Americans go, Sirrí assured me, the Russians will come in their place. Sirrí also had fine Swiss chocolates in a silver bowl which she offered me when I visited her. She was an aristocrat. An elegant lady.

47

The story is always somewhere else. I imagine a book that pretends to tell an official story. In the margins there is another story. It is incidental, it has little bearing on the official story, but that is where the real book is.

The ideal reader, James Joyce said, *who suffers from an ideal insomnia.* The reader is unable to sleep because in the other story there is something wrong. It is a detective story. The reader thinks the enemy must be found. There are clues. They must be pieced together.

The solution is contained in the clue.

Has anyone been murdered?

48

It was not a country where murders took place.

There was development. Geothermal energy had been tapped. Greenhouses were built in the village of Hveragerdi. Fruits and vegetables were cultivated in the greenhouses. Tomatoes, cucumbers, oranges, bananas. There were not enough to go around, and the produce was expensive, but it was a beginning.

I went with my mother and her friend in a jeep to Hveragerdi. She had saved enough money for a bag of tomatoes. We drove for what I thought was a long time, perhaps an hour or two, and went into the greenhouse. There was a sulphuric smell in the air. The scent of the plants was strong and spicy. It was a jungle of plants I had never seen, never known existed.

My mother bought her tomatoes and we drove back. She let me hold the bag as we drove. I sat in the back seat alone while the two women talked in front. I opened the bag and smelled the small dark red tomatoes. It was an overwhelming sweet smell that went into my head and down my throat. Gripped by an irresistible urge to eat one tomato, I surreptitiously swallowed the bites soundlessly. There were many, so I ate another. And another.

When we got home my mother discovered the empty bag. I stole out of the car shamefully. I was afraid she would scold me. Instead she started to cry.

49

Perhaps she thought her life was taking on a hopeless air. It had happened before.

She told me, sometime later, about the strawberries. When she was a young girl, she picked strawberries one summer to earn money. Her family was not wealthy, and she wanted to have a record of some beloved music. It was strenuous work, bending down for many hours, day after day, filling baskets with red berries. In the end she bought her record. On the way home she fell and the record broke.

Many years later I wrote a poem about that pathetic incident. It happened in Denmark, where new strawberries grow every summer.

50

There were records in our house. She must have bought the record again. I imagined it lay stacked among the others.

Sometimes I came home from school and found my father in the living room pretending to work. The table was spread with pieces of paper containing incomprehensible calculations. He was sitting in front of them, pencil in hand, looking at the old record player. There was a heavy record on the turntable, turning, and the loud music filled the whole house. It was always Hungarian gypsy music.

51

If there is a murder it will be somewhere on that American Base, where cumbersome dark green Air Force planes are landing in the fog.

There are stories where everything that is written is a clue.

52

There is nature, which levels all emotions.

When my sister and I slept on the heath, we woke many times during the night, thinking it was dawn. But it was the midnight sun. In the morning we washed our faces in the ice-cold water of the creek. It rushed along its shallow channel bed, over the thick grasses, the water pure and clean. We walked across the heath, jumping over tufts of grass-grown sod, and up the red mountain that loomed over us. It must have been stone that was rich in minerals, for the rocks shone brilliant orange and red as the sun emerged. There were no bushes or grassy patches on the mountain, but on the summit I happened on a few Alpine flowers. Somehow they grew out of cracks in the stone.

I only knew a few flowers by name then. Forget-me-nots, buttercups. Clovers, daisies, dandelions. The common flowers usually considered weeds in other countries. There are times when the English names give no indication of the true nature of these weeds. Or of what I thought was a transcendent quality, given the harsh conditions. The name for buttercup in that country is: island of the sun. Or, the sun that never disappears.

Much later in life I contrived a poetics of naming. Only that which is named is able to live in language. But I did not know many names at the time of my earliest discoveries. It was before language.

Words are not what they signify. We confuse the signifier with the signified. Words are only words. They live in an atmosphere of their own.

Words are suitcases crammed with culture. I imagine a story of emptied containers. Bottles drained of their contents. Travel bags overturned, old clothes, medicine bottles, walking shoes falling all over the airport floor. To come to your destination with nothing in hand. To come to no destination at all.

53

All stories are romances. Detective stories, spy thrillers, horror tales are all romances. They are not real. The romance of the threat. The male romance.

I have heard speakers on the female romance. Sentimentality. Emotion. Feelings of love. Fears of rejection.

I imagine a story that is not a romance.

54

You are contained in the things you love, she said, H.D. said.

55

At times I think we have outgrown the story. We are no longer entertained by pretense. There is too much knowledge. Too much self-consciousness. There are always other stories, metastories, about which we have made an industry. Degrees are offered, awards given, livelihoods supported for the deciphering of metastories.

When we recognize that all our stories are pretense, we run out of enemies. When we run out of enemies, all we have left is love. If it is not love, it is a nothingness. A staring at the snowflakes coming down.

A story that does not desire pretense must incorporate its own metastories.

56

In Rungsted, Denmark, we lived on the upper floors of an enormous estate. The park around the building shed itself in layers of all manner of refined flowers and bushes all the way down to the sea. From that shore it was possible to see the lights of Sweden on the other side of the channel. On one side the estate carried a tower from which it was possible to survey the stars. A narrow spiral staircase wound up to the room in the tower where there was a large telescope.

We understood that a prowler was loose in the area. Do not wander too far along the beach. Do not find yourself alone in the park. My sister and I were alone, trying to sleep in the bedroom beside the balcony. Our parents had taken the train into Copenhagen for the evening. We lay in silence in the dark and heard the prowler climbing onto the balcony. His shadow appeared on the wall, flanked by moonlight.

There is nothing in these rooms for a thief to aspire to own. A few tedious objects from the Arctic, carried in a small wooden trunk on a passenger ship. Schoolbooks in another language. Two white Inuit girls, one of them apprehensive.

57

I knew the Rungsted beach very well. It was different from the Fossvogur beach in Iceland, where our stranded tanker lay waiting for us every morning. Here there was a great deal of driftwood. Pale white angelic pieces of wood washed up out of the water, smooth as healthy skin to the touch. The stones were also smooth and round, often so light grey they seemed white. It was a gentle shoreline, where young girls could walk in white frill dresses carrying baskets with flowers in one hand.

58

Childhood is a time of setting the stage. Later in life you come onto that stage and find it is very hard to change the props.

59

It was James Joyce who said: *the reader wants to steal from the text*. The reader aspires to be a thief. For that reason the text must not be generous.

It is a relief not to have such rules. To play such games. Hide and seek. Not to have rules perhaps means you are free to steal from yourself. Finally.

In Rungsted I joined the prowler in his imagined activities. I stole downstairs into the rooms on the main floor when I knew the old couple was not home. I fingered the gold door handles. I surveyed the crystal vases. The soft porcelain statuettes. The Persian rugs. The velvet upholstered chairs, where the body sank deep in its own reverie. I sat in all the chairs. I thought: it could be that Goldilocks is the bears. Certainly she is the youngest bear. The one who sleeps in her own bed.

As I sat in the heavy gold-rimmed lounging chair in the elegant living room of that estate, I came upon the greatest surprise. On the wall facing the street there was a stained glass window as large as a doorway. It was green and white, illumined by the light of the afternoon. The picture it portrayed was a map of the North: Greenland, Iceland and the Polar Cap.

Much later I read in a medieval love sonnet that the lover's eyes are windows to the soul.

60

Around that time in Hungary, 1956, people were beginning to flee. The Russians had invaded Budapest, and calls for help from the Hungarian revolutionaries, sent in signals to the rest of Europe, went unanswered.

I told him, the one who I think would not want me to write this book, not to be concerned. It is not a book about him. Yet it is a good story, the one he tells. That he was a young boy, the family fled the country separately, one by one. The peasant who was to escort the boy to the Austrian border took him into a large field, pointed in one direction and said: the border is that way. Then he turned and left, and the boy walked on.

Did he know when there was a border? Can borders be felt? Is there perhaps a change of air, a different climate, when you go from one country to another?

That story has bearing on this book only insofar as one is contained in the things one loves.

61

There are in any case people who flee the Russians in an endeavour to become Americans. There are also people who flee the Americans in an endeavour to become Russians.

62

That was the same boy who was put on a Hungarian children's working crew. Those children were not made to grow vegetables. Instead they weeded railroad tracks.

He pulled weeds from railroad tracks all day. His only food was an onion sandwich, which someone else always stole and ate for him.

For that reason he was very thin.

63

A text that is self-deceiving eventually rejects itself. There is always another author, behind the official author, who censors the text as it appears. The other author writes: that is not what you intended to say.

I think of a book that has left in the censor's words. A book that does not pretend it is not talking about itself. All books talk about themselves.

The novel I at one time intended to write rejected itself. It began to talk about its own genesis instead. The story disappeared. In its place there was another story, an unexpected story. A great surprise.

64

In my mother's country there was a great deal of food. At Christmas there was a large family of aunts and uncles and cousins, a large table where all were sitting and many courses brought in by the house-help, one after the other. There were so many courses that my Uncle Hans had to take a break from dinner and smoke a cigarette. I had never seen anyone take a break in the middle of a meal before.

There was also a great deal of music in my mother's country. On the street corners, in the shops, at the train station, people were singing and playing. Families sang before dinner. They sang again after dinner, gathered around the piano.

It was not so happy all the time in Denmark. During the Second World War there were bomb alerts, the lights were out, sirens went off. My mother and father were huddled in the dark along with everyone else. When there were knocks at the door, they were afraid to answer, thinking it would be Germans.

It was during the German occupation of Denmark that Iceland declared its independence. It was known that the Danish army could not easily move in at such a time. However the British army could, so it was a brief moment of independence.

65

The school I went to was in the Sjaelland countryside, a few hours from Copenhagen. It was an old white stone building. I imagined it had been a cloister in the distant past before the Reformation. There was a pond with lilies on the grounds, a number of oaks and willows and birches, and large stretches of manicured lawn.

There were fifty-nine Danish girls in this school and eleven Icelandic ones. The white Inuit girls were not liked because they had packs of dried fish in their rooms and they did not lift their feet properly when they walked. The rumour was that they were too lazy to lift their feet. They bunched up together in the dining room, in the gym, in the halls, and only made friends with each other. They talked about going home again and thought the Danish girls were effete.

The shufflers, as they were sometimes called, did not count me in their group. They thought I was one of the effetes. The effetes did not understand why I was never seen with the shufflers.

The effetes were divided into country and city. The country ones came from farms on Sjaelland.

If their farms still had thatched roofs, and if they drew their water from a water pump in the courtyard, they were lower country. If their farms were wealthy country manors, and the househelp consisted of more than ten people, they were higher country.

The city effetes were similarly divided into slummers and genteels. The slummers were not as high as high country, but they were above the low country girls. They were city dwellers who came from the poorer districts. Sometimes they had illegitimate pregnancies in the very near past, and this was why they were sent to the country school. Sometimes they were thieves. The slummers were respected for being street wise.

The genteels came from well-to-do homes in Copenhagen's enviable districts. Among them there was a minor division of aristocrats and the nouveau riche, with the aristocrats on top. The nouveau riche were daughters of architects and doctors and politicians, about whom there were stories in the press. The aristocrats were daughters of the gentility, whose fathers collected honorary medals and signatures of the king.

This all took a few weeks to iron out. I was the last to be casted because I fell into no category. It took a bit of deliberation. Through some shortcut of the imagination, perhaps because there was a rumour afoot that I was really a Russian, the verdict came down: I was a genteel.

I became an apologist for shufflers. It is not that the shufflers are lazy, I said to the genteels in the back kitchen. They are just tired of this place. They do not like the trees and all this shaved grass. And besides, they cannot stand your politics. You have too many classes here. They come from a classless society, where there are no kings, no counts, no barons. Only occupying armies.

I suspected that one reason for placing me among the elite had more to do with my one-time appearance on American television than with my uncertain Russian ancestry. Several years back I had appeared on American television as a specimen with braids of what the Americans were protecting. There was no knowing, the genteels reasoned, that I would not appear there again.

Much later I realized they could be right. The man I was eventually to marry had been carried in infancy by fleeing parents from North Korea to South Korea. There were Russians in the North, where there was no milk to be had, and there was an American Base in the South, where there was milk. My future mother-in-law was to say to me: if not for American milk, there would have been no husband for you.

66

While I was enjoying these privileges in Denmark, my sister was taking her Student's Examinations in a gymnasium in the mountains in northern Iceland. It was noted that despite the institutionalization of food services to students she was not putting on weight like the rest.

67

There are some things about this Lord-of-the-flies type of sociology, carried out among girls in a rural Danish boarding school, that are not entirely a lie.

That privileges were not dispensed equally. That certain low country girls sat hunched over on their bunks, staring at their toes, while genteel girls freely sunbathed in the nude, within viewing range of the male gardeners. That some slummers loitered around the grocery down the road, in an effort to shoplift, while high country girls had secretive meetings among the tall wheat stalks with young men on bicycles.

It is not exactly a lie that I was free to partake in the activities of all castes. In doing so I acquired an overview of the situation which enabled me to act as advisor on things about which the headmaster and his teachers remained in the dark.

68

There are theorists who say that all stories are lies. All that is written is a lie. There is no such thing as truth.

There are so many people vying for attention in the telling of any given story that they cancel each other out.

I imagine a story that allows all speakers to speak at once, claiming that none of the versions is exactly a lie.

69

The text desires to be true. It knows that what is written is not exactly true, so the desire goes unsatisfied.

The story repeats the attempt at telling itself. The text tells all other texts: there is only one of me.

70

When we were quite young, and I was growing vegetables in the mud, my sister worked for the Forestry Service. The Service's nurseries were located at the bottom of Fossvogur, the fjord on the northern side of our town. Rows of baby pine trees imported from Alaska and northern Norway were taking root in the shallow soil. Only the hardiest trees were imported, the ones able to withstand deprivation.

After my work in the school gardens, I wandered over to the Forestry Service. The miniature branches, lined with soft pine needles, stood wiggling in the constant breeze.

I would eventually find my sister, crouched out of sight in a corner of the nursery. She worked determinedly and did not talk to me when I sat down beside her. I watched her swollen hands, fingers, so disproportionately large on her tiny frame. They were blue with cold. There were open sores that did not heal. They were digging in the dirt, making space for another undersized tree.

71

There is a disagreement about the nature of this story.

There were two radio stations in my father's country. One was the Icelandic National Radio. On that station there was a news hour at noon followed by an hour of advertisements. They played male choirs singing fatherland songs, deep-voiced women singing about mother's beloved eyes, and Viennese waltzes. On Sundays the Bishop addressed the nation with a sermon, and church choirs sang verses from the Hymns of Passion.

The other station was for American servicemen only, but the populace of the island was able to tune in at will. There announcers with Brenda Lee voices said sweet things in English, and American rock music went on all day. If you were caught listening to the American station, you were thought to have silently deserted the tribe. Rolls of invisible barbed wire circled the American Base across the airwaves.

Because there is an American radio station, which the populace can tune in to at will, it is possible that this is a crime story.

It is also possible that what we have here is social realism.

72

On the other hand it is much more likely that this is a love story.

It is about that Hungarian boy who walked through a border that could not be felt. It must be like walking through a cloud of nuclear dust. The dust cannot be seen, felt, heard or smelled, but it lodges in you and makes you susceptible to diseases much later in life.

Somehow he made his way to a refugee camp in Austria. There he earned a few coins by helping an old goldsmith translate documents into English. Or was it a violin maker? He did this for a while, or until the old man began to realize that the boy was translating everything wrong.

73

There was no food in Hungary then. His mother was so tired of not having food that she sent the boy to a relative who owned a farm. Certainly there would be food on a farm.

74

There are, I have come to understand, prowlers everywhere. They prowl about, looking for dialogue. They look for threads.

I do not want to shirk the responsibility of joining in the search for threads. I know there are a few, but it is in the nature of things that the threads be kept out of sight. Or be only barely discernible. Yet they are quite obvious.

The text admits: this is how I am sewn together.

75

Few people are as discriminating as prowlers who are thieves. They are exacting and have high standards.

Hansel and Gretel knew they should leave a considered trail of crumbs behind them as they went through the woods so they could steal from themselves on their way back. They were hoping the trail would not be eaten by birds.

76

In another version of the story of Hansel and Gretel, the two children come from opposite directions through the woods. They meet at the house made of sugar and gingerbread, where an old woman is baking things in an oven. Besides sugar and gingerbread, that house has a television, a radio, Disneyland tinsel toys and candy in shining wrappers.

77

Kjartan was one of the few people on the island in the Arctic who owned a violin. He was also one of the few who knew how to play it. He practiced the instrument in the late afternoons when it was already dark outside. He was in the kitchen, the doors were closed and the lights were off. When I stayed at his house, I was allowed to sit in the corner of the dark kitchen and listen to him play.

It was not entirely dark. There was light coming in through the window from the outside, and I could see his shadow playing.

78

When the British soldiers departed from my father's country, they left a number of empty army barracks behind. There were clusters of these barracks that comprised barrack villages east of town, west of town, and also north and south of town.

At that time there was an invasion of rural people into the city. There was no longer food to be had on the farms, and there were too many mouths to feed. These people moved into the empty barracks, where the city allowed them to stay until better solutions could be found. The barrack villages were sorry places, where rats were frequently seen dashing from one iron-clad shack to another.

The white Inuit had no experience of slums before this. They did not know what had come upon them. Whatever it was, barrack dwellers became the social outcasts of the world's first classless society.

79

At one time we lived close to the barrack village that was located west of town. The slum quarter began only a few houses away, and we were made to understand that those people were segregated from us. As I went about on my street, testing the depth of brown mud puddles, I wondered whether they were lepers. Or perhaps all tubercular.

Inevitably I acquired a friend from the barracks. She took me home to see her house, and I was careful to leave no clues as to where I was going. Inside there was hardly any furniture. It was somehow nondescript. It was an interior not easily remembered. A non-house.

The barrack she lived in contained no bathroom. I asked her: where do you bathe? In the fjord, she said. I went with her to the shore soon afterwards, and she took me to a secluded spot where the water from the sea was pooled quietly between two boulders. There were no swimsuits then, so we took off our clothes and swam naked in the stilled dark seawater.

80

All the memories gathered in the text are sorry ones.

The text acknowledges its own sorrow. It does not seek an apology for its own transparency.

When we were bathing in the fjord, the barrack-girl and I, an American soldier suddenly appeared behind the rocks. He stood looking at us for a while, and I carefully deliberated what to do next. We were perhaps eleven or twelve then. The young man said to me in American English: I've lost my watch. Would you help me find it?

81

I have sometimes thought: it is possible there is no such thing as chronological time. That the past resembles a deck of cards. Certain scenes are given. They are not scenes the rememberer chooses, but simply a deck that is given. The cards are shuffled whenever a game is played.

The same game may be played several times. Each time the game is played the configurations are different, and a new text emerges.

I imagine a text that refuses to play its own game.

82

There was a conspiracy among the kids in my school to boycott the Danish lessons. The boycott was to consist of a refusal to do the homework. We were all to appear at our desks at the set time, and when the teacher calls us up to recite our homework, no one is able to say the lesson.

I did not know whether the boycott took place because no one liked the Danish teacher or whether it was a political act. If we were no longer a colony of Denmark, it could be reasoned, then Danish should be removed from the curriculum.

The Danish teacher's name was Óli. He called us up to say the lesson, beginning with the first desk. The first offered the excuse that he had not done the homework. The second did the same, and the third and fourth. He went from desk to desk and got the same answer each time.

After a while Óli walked back to his desk slowly, stood with his back to us, spread out his arms and pressed his fingers into the blackboard. He waited for several minutes until he commenced another try. He walked up to my desk, knowing I would be able to say the lesson. After all, I already spoke Danish.

I did not say a word, but stared him directly in the face. He knew as well as I that it was no longer a language class. It was a kind of cold war. The object of a cold war must be, I thought as we stared each other down, to ascertain who your enemies are.

It was a long silence. At the end of it Óli picked up his briefcase and walked out of the room. I detected a note of triumph in his exit. There are some people, he seemed to insinuate, who are their own enemies.

83

I did not have the proper Tin-drummish distance required for a story.

Materials for stories came from magical places so far away that people there had never heard of us. The Russian steppes and the Hungarian plains and the Chinese mountains. But for us way up here in the North there never would be a story.

84

There was another boarding school, a small one. This was in the mountains, an hour from Reykjavík, and it contained both boys and girls. It was understood that passing the National Exams was hard work, and it could not be done in an environment where students went on strike in order to change the curriculum.

The headmaster, who had sole authority over twenty still half-incubating souls, took the opportunity to use the dormitory as a training ground for young communists. This was done with directive speeches in the evenings, unswerving discipline and the availability of instructive books.

85

There were things about his theories I liked. Such as: in that ideal world it was possible to be what you were, for no one would care. There would be no need for hunger strikes against God.

I was still looking for an argument to present to my sister. There had been many hospital visits, and I was not pleased with the voice that had nothing to say. If only the right argument could be found, I reasoned, she would acquire another view and the cold war between her, my parents and God would end.

86

The dining room of that school doubled as a library. That was done in order to make the books easily visible. Students would walk by these books at least six times a day, to and from meals. It was hoped they would sometimes stop and read something.

If this was a trap, I was an easy prey. It was a collection of books from and about the places in the world that most fascinated me. Here, I realized, was an opportunity to find out what exactly went on there. No more illusions, no more emotional clap-trap. No more distressed lovers suffering the ironies of fate. No more gypsy fiddlers and women in blue dancing in passionate circles. No more Chinese emperors with fake songbirds that break down at all the wrong moments.

Soon I became a noted prowler in the library. When study hour was strictly enforced, which it was whenever we were not eating or exercising, and young people sat in their rooms bent over their books, checked on every twenty minutes by the headmaster himself making his rounds, I was found in the library, blithely reading. It was a point of pride, I realized, for the headmaster to have caught me in his trap. For that reason he did not discipline me. He walked by me on his rounds oblivious to the lack of regimentation I presented him with. Sometimes he stopped to inquire what I was reading, then he patted the top of my head and went away.

I was reading Malraux. *Man's Fate*. The Revolution in China. Here was something worth writing about. That was certainly a story.

87

I did not know that only one year later I would find myself in an American high school, faced with the ponderously difficult task of pledging allegiance to the American flag.

In the American high school all students were ushered into the auditorium first thing in the mornings. There was an order to stand up, place your right hand over your heart and recite the pledge. I stood up with hundreds of others, turned to face the flag as it went up, but neglected to cover my heart, and I did not know the litany. I needed, I told the others in poor English, more time to think about it.

88

There I was free to associate with American soldiers before they became soldiers. There would be no stigma attached to such an association. I was told that if I ever found a Central European in that place, unlikely as it would be, he would certainly be the reactionary kind.

Whatever cardhouses I had been building in my imagination, they tumbled overnight. The voice that was about to press its case to its sister retreated again into a non-voice. At that time I wrote my first story.

89

The text has a desire to censor the stories it does not love.

Because of that it is impossible that this is a love story.

If I were not full of love there would be no words on the page. There would be no text, no book.

90

You kill what bothers you, Roland Barthes said.

I imagine a text that does not kill.

There were after all tiny Alpine flowers at the top of the red mountain my sister and I climbed. I did sit down on the stone summit, blown naked by the tireless wind, and look at the flower in the crack. From that vantage point I had a view of the entire heath below, and of a valley of red stone, a thin creek meandering into the sea, and beyond, the sea itself. When I spoke, an echo resounded in the rock face behind me, repeating itself over and over, throwing itself from one wall to the other.

I thought I understood, in a slow dawning of the senses, why it was that my father's people thought stones and water and wind and ocean were alive. Inhabited.

Everything, I told myself, depends on the vantage point.

All that a story is, I thought, is a way of looking at things.

91

It is said that you should not pick those Alpine flowers, for it takes each one twenty-five years to grow. If you pick it you will be snuffing out twenty-five years.

92

My sister, like me, went away for a while to an educational institution. I did not know what it was like there. She told me nothing. At the end of the year, we all came back. It was summer, there were small birds trying to chirp in the homegrown bushes in the small yard. They were starting to spend the night chirping, confused about the midnight sun.

My sister did not walk in, but knocked faintly on the door instead. It was my mother who opened the door. It must have been her, for it was not my father, and I do not remember being the first to see the apparition in the doorway. Whoever it was, my sister stood on the front steps, barely able to stand up. She was no larger than her own skeleton. She was as thin as anyone could get.

Her eyes were large, her lips were blue and she had trouble holding her head up. There was a crisis in the house. She was carried in, put onto the bed, God's name was called in what must have been vain and someone said, probably my mother: why did not anyone tell us?

The bedside vigils began again. There were doctors, talk of hospitals. I sat down beside her and found I had become afraid of this lonely resistance of hers. There was nothing I could say that would change what was in front of me. Yet I thought there must be something I could say if I knew what it was. It was a matter of outlook. Some pattern into which the story could fall.

Those magic words I did not have. If there are magic words they must all be far away.

93

The writer cannot escape repression. The text represses the writer. The text is the writer's prison.

The words will not take the writer into themselves. The author is therefore locked out of the book.

94

It was not a country where children were asked: what is your name? Instead we were asked: who owns you? The proper answer for this is: my father owns me.

The kindly shoesmith thought I resembled someone he knew. It was in the shop I passed when I took shortcuts home from school and went through the alley. I always stopped at the shoesmith's because I liked the smell of leather. The man in the brown apron said: who owns you? My father, Gunnar Bödvarsson.

I took these forms of expression literally. I was certain I was my father's property. As property I had the right to speak to him on occasion. Such occasions did not come up with my mother, whom I was less related to.

95

The self-reflective text desires to be a comedy.

In that other version of the Hansel and Gretel story, the birds were awake all night and ate the crumbs lying in the woods. The boy and girl discovered they had lost their trail.

The text desires to laugh at itself. To make the pattern come out happily. Or at least to let the pattern show up in a good light.

The story knows the pattern is given. There are some things it cannot change. It would like to be free to rewrite itself. To surpass itself.

There is a certain acknowledgment in this writing that there is an itinerary. A *set*. A kind of fidelity is desired.

96

The structure never can close. It is always violated from inside by the writer who is locked in. Before there is a text the writer is imprisoned inside. After the text appears the writer is exiled from it. On both sides there are violations.

There are days when the story deserts me. Usually on overcast days, if the winter is too mild. The idea that the consciousness is free to begin again, to disregard what has gone before, presents itself. I notice an urge to stare the past down. To be haughty towards it, speak to it from a position of strength. The word I have an urge to say is: traitor!

The story is likewise arrogant. It talks back, claiming for itself a certain autonomy. The story tells its exponent: you do not know me.

97

In another version of my childhood, I did not grow up in my parents' house at all. When I was not in school I lived with another family. A childless couple whose house stood by itself in the bottom of the fjord.

In that house I had my own bed. It was an alcove in the wall, in what they called the north-east room, in the loft. From the window of that room it was possible to see the entire fjord as it spread out to the open sea. The stranded tanker lay below, close by, and I could keep an eye on the tide. Above, a large new cemetery was being unearthed.

There were times when I was asked to return to my parents' house. When I was putting on my jacket and shoes, getting ready to go home, I allowed myself to feel that I was being turned out of my home and sent to stay the night with strangers.

98

In the metatext there is an acknowledgment that the consciousness is *turned out* wherever it desires to settle.

99

The names of the childless couple I lived with were Hanna and Palli. They painted their house red and their address was: The Red House.

It is a curious story that suppresses its own happiness.

In the Red House I woke in the mornings while it was still dark. It would be winter, and daylight would not begin until just before noon. I crawled out of my alcove among the model ships and oil paintings of sailing vessels. There was a smell of coffee somewhere, and an oil-burning stove.

I went downstairs. There was only one small lamp glowing in the corner of the living room, and most of the house was dark except for the kitchen. When I came down I found Hanna walking about in her underwear, very surprised to see me. She was Danish and said ridiculous things for an adult, crass and funny.

100

Since they could not have children, they at one time thought they might adopt. So they went to an orphanage to find a child of their own. While they were there, a red-haired boy ran up to Hanna and called: mom. For some reason they decided against adoption and remained content just being two. But there was always that image of the red-haired boy.

All the stories deliberately collected have notes of regret in them. A touch of wishfulness, that the story were describing an alternative world.

I looked for red hairs in the mirror. I wanted to occupy the space left open by regret.

101

It is possible to be so full of love that the voice that is inundated with words is unable to speak.

The simplest words clamour to get out, but all that emerges is silence.

This is the voice that sits beside hospital beds. The voice that cannot see clearly which configuration of words will be the one to remove all the rolls of barbed wire.

Love seeks refuge in figurative language. Love is ashamed of itself, of its own transparency. It is vulnerable territory. A people without its own army, easily occupied by armed forces of other nations.

Love turns itself out.

102

The problem of Dr Patel, who came from India, was never resolved. I worried that he might find it offensive watching us eat the meat of a whale. If I had been allowed to speak, I would have said: the white Inuit take what comes in its own season.

103

There is a reason for the scarcity of stories. Of cards in the deck. Aside from the tendency stories have to repress themselves in their desire to fall in with dogma.

There was much illness. Large patches of months and years were blotched out. A kind of ink stain appeared in the text, where the consciousness became obliterated. It was not exactly unconsciousness that took over, but a state of exhausted ennui. A desire to forget.

The ink stains did not always have names. Often they were called the flu, or they bore the titles of common childhood illnesses. On one occasion it was a form of typhoid fever. On another occasion it was suspected of being polio. But most of them were just there, frequent collapses, a way of life.

104

They were times when I lay semiconscious, vaguely aware that an unknown hand was examining glands or listening to heartbeats with a stethoscope. Voices of the doctor and my mother could be heard above me, coming as if from a great distance. When I opened my eyes there would be faces bent over me, usually bearing an expression of helpless concern.

Times when I found myself on a cold floor in the middle of the night. The familiar ring in my ears, announcing the appearance of some alien force arriving to retrieve me. Slowly I knew I was disappearing. It did not cause me much concern. Everyone else was far too fussy, I thought.

Those who are disappearing are far wiser than those who sit by the bedside. There were times

I wanted to reassure the faces that I was simply taking a break. But I was not always able to fetch my voice from that great distance. It seemed like a phenomenally long way to go, down somewhere in an area of wet ocean caverns, where my voice was lodged for a while.

105

That is an area where there is a cessation of stories. If death is another play after the one about life, it must like all good plays have rehearsals. The consciousness rehearses an existence without stories.

It is in the nature of writing to contain a note of defiance. To confront its opposite, to stare it down. To make a certain claim for life.

It is also a confrontation that looks in, for what is being defied is located inside writing. A form of cold war, where the ink that is directed into patterns is carefully watched so it will not spill over and spread out, uncontrolled.

106

My mother, who had been brought up in Copenhagen, could not exactly resign herself to her new home on a mountainous island in the North. She had many reasons for taking her two daughters back to her own city and did so frequently. I did not inquire what the reasons were, but let myself be taken back and forth. There was not much to choose between.

There were ocean crossings. The ship that sailed us to and fro was called Gullfoss and was an old trusty passenger ship of fairly small proportions. When I lived on it, however, it was as large as any other world I knew.

We lived on the Gullfoss so often that I had perpetual sea legs, even after we had been on land for weeks. It was natural that the floor should tilt in different directions. That curtains should extend themselves horizontally. That all loose objects should be securely fastened to the wall. Even on land I watched carefully to make sure that plates and cups would not slide from the table.

The Gullfoss was the only place where I loved loneliness. There was the loneliness of the heavy ocean that extended in black billows as far as the eye could see, day after day. The loneliness of having nothing to do and being fascinated by that nothingness. Of being in a world without expectations, where the body was simply being carried forward in an environment where forward and backward did not exist.

Sometimes we saw land. It would be Scotland or the Faeroe Islands or Denmark, a thin blue streak in the distance at which people pointed. I resented land when it appeared. I did not want to come near those masses of stone, where people paraded in streets with small paper flags on flimsy sticks. I conceived of a desire to belong to the sea. To have been born on a ship. There were attempts at rewriting history.

I began to understand the addiction of fishermen to the ocean. It became my ambition to be a seaperson. I went about with private convictions.

107

An anonymous person on board had taken an entire table in the lounge to himself, on which a puzzle was in the process of being pieced together. It was not clear what the picture represented exactly. The images resembled an impressionistic painting or some undefined Monet waterlilies.

I never saw the owner at work on his puzzle. We speculated, my sister and I, who it might be and narrowed the candidates down to the First Mate and the Captain. He only worked on it at night, for the puzzle made no progress during the day. But in the mornings we came into the lounge and discovered whole new sections in the picture. The man with the puzzle was a nightwalker. We called him the prowler.

108

I decided to join the prowler in the compilation of puzzle pieces. During the day I sat over the impossible lack of clarity and affixed a few pieces together after great deliberation. At night the prowler added to what I had done. A kind of communication between us ensued.

We had a joint project at which we took shifts. The project was to clarify the picture. To make the patterns emerge out of a random *set*.

When the puzzle was almost finished, I saw it must have been a Monet. Something French. But we had rough seas, and one morning I found the tediously arranged picture on the floor, again in shambles. No one had the stamina to begin it again.

109

Much later in life I found myself in an art school. We were instructed in self-portraiture. Our task was to work from a mirror in oil on canvas. The mirror was affixed to the top of the easel, so the face in the portrait was looking up. A picture emerged of a disinterested face with dark blond hair. I did not like the project. It was beside the point.

110

It was a long time before I understood that the point is an illusion. That portraits occur without center. In a puzzle every piece is its own center, and when compiled the work is either made up entirely of centers or of no center at all.

In the metastory there are figurative prowlers looking for something. But there is very little for them to find.

On the ship my sister and I amused ourselves with jokes. Where is the best place to put something you don't want a person to find? On top of his own head.

The prowler does not know he already has what is being sought.

111

The reader is new to being a hero. He is not used to this spotlight, to having books named after him.

I conceived of another sort of self-portrait: the painter paints her own image, but paints it directly on the mirror. The viewer sees not the image of the artist, but his own face through the lines of oil paint. The face looking back at the viewer will have an expression of helpless concern.

112

In my father's country it was necessary for all people to work. Men worked on the trawlers. Women worked in the fish plants. Children worked in the school gardens. Young boys carried newspapers on the streets, yelling the headlines. Young girls were put in charge of infants while their mothers were in the fish. There were playgrounds where children were confined within concrete walls.

Slogans were written large on the buses that drove by: *Let us build the nation.*

I was in the fish plant and cannery that had been built in the west end of my town. The building was by the water, below the settlement of houses that stood on an incline. My task was to put cans of fish into cardboard boxes. I arranged cans in that square space all day. It was non-work. I did not like it. At the end of the day I did not remember where I had been. The natural world, with its sunsets and blank waters, became an alien place.

It was understood that patience was a great virtue.

113

My sister was sent up north to a fishing hamlet called Raufarhöfn. There she was to stand on the wharf, wearing an oilskin apron and waterproof gloves, and arrange herring between layers of salt into large barrels. The herring were to be eviscerated and salted as soon as the boats brought them in. An army of workers was required to barrel the herring while still fresh.

There were sixteen hour days. When she went to her bunk, exhausted, she lay down to sleep, not always bothering to take her shoes off. There would be a few hours of dozing, then the bell would ring again to announce another boat. Everyone went out again and continued barrelling.

114

Those were the summer months. Schools dismissed children early in the spring so they could join the work force. Many went into the country and raked hay in the field.

Children did not play summer games. They went to the places where they were to spend the night, after working during the day, and put their heads on kitchen tables and chair backs. They were found crumpled up in corners and curled up on floors.

Adults did not enter into the picture. Adults were not there. They were doing two, sometimes three, jobs. After one work there was another work, and there were many shifts that came in rows.

Parents turned into rumors. Families became hearsay. Children went about adopting makeshift families and surrogate relatives. The farmer and his wife. The captain on the boat. The shift supervisor in the factory. New parents.

There was an adage that said: *Work as the day is long.* I do not remember there being any night. After all it was summer.

115

Happiness was beside the point.

Happiness could only be found in what you did. It was a non-happiness. An acceptance. A certain sorrow.

Children became cultivators of love. To love the sheep, to love the calves, the horses, the fish. Even as they were consumed. To love the people who were there. A certain longing.

I refused to go home when I came out of the fish plant. It was a silent house. There was no presence in the rooms. The kitchen counter was cleared and blank. The beds were empty. The living room door was closed, and there was no one on the other side of the door. It was a space, but an uninhabited space.

I went to other houses. Wherever there was a person at home. I realized in a slow dawning way that it was a country whose most notable product was love. I loved in a longing and sorry way the person who gave me a bowl of soup. Or a place to sleep. An alcove in the wall. The person who was at home when I walked in unannounced.

116

The question of the murder remained.

In Rungsted, where there were gold door handles and a stargazing tower, there had been a murder recently. A young girl was found on the shore, near the entrance to our garden park that went on up the incline in layers of flowers. It was not known whether the prowler, whose presence had been noted at odd times, was also the murderer, or whether there were actually two criminals wandering about.

There was a hint of *apprehension* in the air, a note of *warning*. Yet I could not resist the beach. I made my way down to the water, careful not to leave any clues as to my whereabouts, and snuck through the gate just above the sand. The sand was white. I was not used to white sand, and it was warm. The water lapped the shore gently, as if trying not to wake the stones and driftwood.

117

When I was in Copenhagen, I stayed with my great-aunt. She lived on a broad and busy street. I slept on her sofa, and all night I heard noises of the city. Cars went by tirelessly. A train passed through distant train yards. There were buses and cable cars. Kids on bicycles. Whistles, horns blowing.

In the morning the househelp brought out coffee. It was a young woman whose special domain was the kitchen. It was not considered well mannered for me to go into the kitchen, for it was her area. I observed her from the distance of invisible social barricades.

I was not used to city noises. I was not used to class differences within homes either. It seemed so arbitrary, who worked for whom. I did not love my great-aunt's house. The formality of silver spoons and crystal glasses.

118

My great-aunt Sirrí, in my father's country, imitated those Danish ways. She was, or so it was rumored, upper crust, so she had househelp in the kitchen as well. But that was an elderly Icelandic woman with large breasts and a warm smile. I spent my time on a stool in the kitchen, listening to her talk, watching her wash dishes. She was laughing.

I noticed my father's people could not play the game they were supposed to play without laughing. They made fun of themselves.

119

It was a time when the pattern was not yet clear. Stories had only begun. There had been no development of plots, no interweaving of incidents, no coincidences had meshed. There were no endings in sight.

I could afford a view of the world that was constructed out of simple chance. There was no order to history. Fate took random turns.

The longer you live, I thought much later in life, the more deliberate the pattern that emerges seems to be. If it is God's story, I considered, then it must be waited for. It is a story that is read in time. It is not my story. The author is unknown. I am the reader.

120

The writer is a prowler in a given story that emerges in time. The writer reports on incidents. There are no protagonists in the given story. Any subject is a contrived subject. The point of view is uncertain. The writer is necessarily part of the story.

The writer cannot report on everything. It is not necessary to tell the whole story. There will be just enough to provide a faint sketch of the pattern.

In any case the writer expects rough seas. The entire work may find itself on the floor in the end, again in shambles.

121

There was an imprint in those early years. I was looking for that imprint already in childhood. It was a face. I did not know whose it was, but someone looked at me and left an imprint.

I have read works on the psychology of early childhood. The face, I read, is usually that of the mother. Or the father. But I do not think the face belonged to my parents. It belonged to another person whose name I have forgotten.

Perhaps it was the First Mate on the Gullfoss as we sailed to Copenhagen. The one who dispensed the medicines on board. He came to my cabin. I lay in my bunk, ill, not entirely conscious. The First Mate was speaking with my mother. He said to her: it is possible you have not escaped the polio epidemic in Reykjavík in time. I opened my eyes in time to see his face. He was injecting penicillin into my arm.

122

There is a first face, and then there is a second face. The second is not the same as the first, but very similar.

It is necessary to undergo the loss of the first face. The consciousness seeks to retrieve the first image in the second. It is a longing that cannot be fulfilled.

The actual fulfillment of such a desire would in any case be a shattering experience. The consciousness is content with the lover's unfulfilled desire.

In literature, I found in later years, the first face is often confused with the face of God.

123

The writer is given to resorting to differently coloured light bulbs. To placing the story in an inappropriate light. For that reason this is a story about the North Atlantic Treaty Organization.

124

I had a certain friend in the town between the two fjords who was different from the rest. Her hair was quite black and straight. Her skin was darker, more golden, and her eyes were dark brown. She was not considered pretty. There was a lack of proportion there. She was too short, the nose was too big, her face too narrow. It was a country of intense homogeneity, and any variation was noticeable.

Her father, it was rumored, was an American soldier. But she did not go to America and she did not speak English, so she escaped the jeers of other kids that were reserved for apparent foreign sympathizers. She lived with her mother and an older brother, who was quite normal. There was no father in the house.

Her name was Álfhildur. Her mother belonged to a religion that was termed Elf-Belief. Elf-Belief consisted of a certain faith in the healing powers of elves. When Álfhildur was dangerously ill, her mother contacted the elves. During the night, while she slept, the elves injected some extraordinary substance into her arm, and she recovered.

Álfhildur claimed she was faintly conscious of the presence of the elves in the night.

125

I had another friend whose name was Sigrún. There was a curse on Sigrún's family. Among the many children born to the parents, those who did not die suffered from some deformity or other. The rumour was that it had been a marriage of siblings who themselves had perhaps been conceived by siblings.

It was a small country, with a small tribe of people. Repetitions were bound to occur. It was understood.

At last there were only Sigrún and her father left in the house. When her father suddenly died, she locked herself in her room and refused to come out. Some relative had moved in and was making sure she was fed and clothed. No one saw Sigrún for a few weeks. We did not dare guess how she felt.

When she was ready to talk to someone again, she sent for me. I went to her house, feeling uncertain. When I arrived I was ushered into her room by a woman who said: I am so glad you came. Sigrún was on the floor. She grabbed my legs and told me her father had appeared to her in a dream and spoken to her. She was crying.

I sat down on the floor with her. Perhaps, I thought, even though I have nothing to say to her, perhaps just being here is enough.

126

It is possible, I thought as we held on to each other on that floor, that even this has political roots.

At school, as we sat with our open school-books in front of us, there was talk of what was called the Danish trade monopoly. The white Inuit were prevented from leaving the island and prevented from trading with other nations. As a result there was not enough food. The population decreased.

Faces, I was made to understand, began to repeat themselves with greater frequency.

127

When I was twelve I fell in love for the first time. The object of my affection was a twelve year old boy with yellow hair that always fell into his eyes. We were the best of friends. He came to fetch me at six in the evenings, and we prowled the streets together until after eleven. We were fond of fences and rooftops, and contrived various ways of climbing over things. We were also fond of open windows, into which well-aimed snowballs could be flung.

His name was Siggi, and we had in common a great love of wooden shoes. At that time we lived in what was called the old town, where the streets bore the names of Nordic gods. There was a street for Thor, for Odin, for Frey, for Loki, and so on. Our house was situated on the one dedicated to Thor. Siggi lived a few houses away, on the same street, in an old wooden building with lace curtains and porcelain statuettes on the windowsill. I had a great desire to see the inside of that house.

The old town had been constructed according to a Danish model. There were several storeys to each building, and they were attached by fences that opened into dome-shaped tunnel entrances. As you entered these openings, you found yourself in a courtyard with several windows looking down at you on all sides. Siggi and I had been passively adopted as the prowlers of these courtyards.

When we moved out of the old town into the village between the two fjords, I lost sight of my friend.

128

Almost four years later there was the annual Independence Day celebration in the city. It was the day before we were to travel to America. I went downtown to join in the dancing. Musicians were playing on the street corners, and people filled the streets, dancing and singing. It was a night in June when it never got dark, and the festivities were attended as usual with a good deal of drink.

Since I had been away at educational institutions, I no longer belonged to a city clique and did not participate in the drinking. I was about to go home when someone grabbed my arm and said: if it isn't you! When I turned around I saw a young fellow with yellow hair still in his eyes.

I had a vague sense of an odd pattern emerging. It is possible, I thought, that such threads, apparently disappeared, reemerge at unexpected moments.

I did therefore get to see the inside of Siggi's house just in time. It was a small home, with aged heavy furniture. Downstairs Siggi had his own room, where there was a fluffy eiderdown quilt on the bed. So I did have a place to sleep on the last night in that country.

129

There are stories that appear as dead ends. They go nowhere. They are knots in the fabric. The text would like to censor the dead-end stories.

Behind this desire lies a tacit acknowledgment that some stories matter and others do not. It is not certain what makes one story more significant than another. Perhaps it is a connection, a hint in the story that there is a relation in it to a broader perspective.

I have noticed in a passive way that in literature, as well as in politics, only that which kills is thought significant. Only murder is taken seriously.

It is because the white Inuit do not murder that they are forgotten. They are the harmless people. The insignificant ones. There is no price on people of peace. It costs nothing to eliminate them.

130

If, as D.H. Lawrence claimed, violence is perverted sex, brought about by unfulfilled desire, then the absence of violence presupposes a certain kind of sexual satiation.

131

Some stories claim significance for themselves without appearing to be correct. The writer tacitly submits to the insistence and fetches the story, usually from some vague preconscious era.

Memories of early childhood do not come easy. There is only a sense of warmth, and all recollections run together. They appear on a kind of drying paper, where the ink seeps out of its channels.

132

When I was five I was allowed to attend a special school that admitted preschool children into the elementary grades. I was in a class of six year olds, and we were being taught the alphabet. Large posters with large letters were placed before us. The principal came to fetch me one day and took me into the hall, where he had put two chairs. We sat down on the chairs, he placed a book on my lap and told me to read from it. I read. When I was done he looked at me very calmly and said: well, what shall we do with you? You already know how to read.

We sat in the hall for what must have been several minutes and just smiled. There was a sense of conspiracy in the air. That he and I shared a trade secret.

133

Eventually English was added to the curriculum of Icelandic schools. Perhaps it was because of the American Base. Perhaps it was an attempt to connect up with at least one, somewhat universal, international trade language.

When English classes started, we were around thirteen. It was discovered, to my own mortification, that I already spoke English. I tried to defend myself. I denied my knowledge of English and said to the others: I don't really know the language, it only seems that way.

I was eyed suspiciously. After some deliberation there was a new name for me. Other kids yelled at me from across the street: American Dane! There were moments of intense humiliation. It was not enough, I thought, for fate to place me in the ranks of our former enemies. Now that the memories of Danish colonization were mellowing out, I was just getting by. But fate has to turn around and join me up with the new colonizers as well.

There was a sense of anger. I studied methods of escape with greater intensity. If familiarity with a language determines a person's identity, I considered, I would learn Russian myself. I unearthed my father's Russian dictionary. I set myself study hours every day.

As time went by an even better idea presented itself. Supposing I were to learn to speak Russian, and then the Russian army would occupy us. It would be digging myself deeper into the hole. The solution was to study more languages. I would learn French and German, Faeroese and Inuit. I would confuse them all.

134

It was not exactly a lie that I did not really know English. It was an elementary knowledge, a seven-year-old English, first-grade vocabulary.

It happened when I was seven. My father decided to spend a year in America at the California Institute of Technology and get himself a Ph.D. This was because, I was told, it would enable him to bring the hot water from under the ground more easily into the buildings and the greenhouses. Such an activity requires knowledge, my father assured me, and they know a good deal about it over there.

The whole family went to live for a year in Pasadena, California. There was a lengthy ocean crossing, during which I felt entirely at home. We sailed into New York harbor past the Statue of Liberty. The air was distinctly hazy and rather dirty.

We crossed the continent on a train. There were nights in the bunk in the sleeper when everything rattled ceaselessly. There were meals in the dining car, where it was possible to sit under the glass dome on top and watch while all kinds of landscape flew by.

135

I did not know I was embarking on a year that I would subsequently attempt to erase.

I gained a vague understanding from my year in America that all stories contain a level of under-erasure. A certain urge to blot themselves out. A fear of imprisonment.

136

It was a remarkable year. There was no illness. And there was no work. America turned out to be a country where girls went to school in dresses and where everyone had televisions that showed Mickey Mouse. There were thirty-one flavors of ice cream in America and a great many palm trees.

137

When we arrived at the house we were to live in, on a broad street in Pasadena, a large number of neighbors suddenly appeared. Ladies brought cookies on paper plates wrapped in cellophane. Men stopped to say hello and show us how the garage door worked. A group of children came to play, but discovered I did not understand them. A conference was held. They disappeared and returned with pictures. We went into the patio. They held up a picture of a cow, and said: cow. I repeated after them.

I could not believe what I was seeing. These incredibly kind people, were they also the ones in the U.S. Air Force trucks that drove by us on the highway in Kópavogur? And the ones in the fighter bombers, rehearsing how to fly overhead? People I had been warned against.

138

For most of that year I remained stubbornly silent. I recognized the English words, but did not let on that I understood. At the school I went to, the teacher was concerned that I was not learning the language. A private tutor was called in. Once a day she came to fetch me from the class. We went into the Principal's office, and she showed me the basics of English. There was a meeting with the principal. I was not learning.

I understood what they said. I thought they were too nervous about this. I just needed to think about a few things. While I was thinking, people were smiling at me a good deal.

139

It was at this time that my sister discovered she was on a collision course with reality.

I found her on a chair in the garden. The sun was shining. There was a warm smoggy haze in the air. She was pondering and said to me: there are going to be inevitable problems.

140

It was also at this time that I made my appearance on American television, which later so fatefully determined my caste in a Danish boarding school.

A studio in Hollywood was looking for someone like me to put on one of their shows. After negotiations with school authorities, I was chosen for the amazing task of standing in front of a camera, holding a can of peanuts and staring uncomprehendingly.

Some studio people arrived at school, fetched me out of class and drove me into Hollywood. We stopped at the television station, and after going through many doors and being fixed up by various hands, I found myself standing on a stage, in front of an audience, in what was called a live show. There were questions about the white Inuit, who were not called the white Inuit there, and how I liked America. I sometimes nodded. There was not much to say.

I was trying to figure out: if this was a live show, what were the dead shows like?

141

Anything that is written necessarily has a point of view. The text refuses to give in to public demand, which insists it either have no point of view or all points of view at once. This is what is called objective. The text is not objective because it is unable to be so and still be a text.

142

Everything that happened in America seemed trivial and not at all part of the real world.

I recognized even then that it is not possible to sympathize with all sides at once. When you choose your allegiances, I thought, you ally yourself with the one who suffers.

143

My parents had come upon an elderly Russian couple in Pasadena. We visited them. They had, I was told, fled their homeland and made their home in California. There were things to eat and drink on the table, and they were talking. Both of them were kindly looking, with very white hair.

The Russian woman found me staring raptly at a doll she had standing on the mantelpiece. It was a small white-haired doll clothed in a long yellow dress. She came up to me and said: this is a Russian costume. Then, after some silence, she took the doll down, handed it to me and said I could have it.

I detected that aura, which I have since identified as love, in the elderly woman's silence. It was an ethereal substance, I had noticed, that was oddly charged with warmth, sorrow and regret. It occurred most often among those who did not speak.

I was to be very fond of that gift and had it with me for thirty years.

144

There are gifts that are gifts and other gifts that are bribes. It later occurred to me that children always know the difference.

145

In my father's country I knew several families where the mother was Danish. It happened because, in the forties, young Icelandic men were still going to Copenhagen for a higher education. There they met beautiful Danish women, married them and brought them home when the war was over.

My mother and her friends kept the group. They met regularly and laughed a great deal when they did.

Among them there was a Jewish woman who did not laugh as much. She had, I was told, lost her mother and a sister in a concentration camp. When Jews were being rounded up in Copenhagen, one of my father's friends married this woman, giving her the immunity of an Icelandic citizen.

I thought of this often when I was still very young. I was taking cues, gathering evidence, collecting clues on the nature of friendship.

146

The text acknowledges that there is a search. The same game is played several times with different results.

In literature, tradition instructs, there is usually a protagonist. The protagonist is always on a journey. If inquiries are made concerning the stories behind the story, the text yields to the pressure and gives up a form of an answer. The object of the search is, we are told, a kind of holy grail.

The quest in literature is a mirror of the quest in life. It is possible to imagine a story where the protagonist is a reader, who is therefore also the author. It is a story where the boundary between that which is written and that which is lived remains unclear.

There never is a holy grail. Instead it is a quality. An undefined substance without physical properties that is generated in certain instances. It appears at odd unexpected moments. Even while the weaving has stopped and the weaver is looking out the window at the snow coming down.

147

When we lived in the old town, on the street named after the god Thor, an old couple resided downstairs. They were Björg, who had long thin grey braids and round cheeks, and Magnús, who was tall and thin. Both of them were always smiling.

Magnús had a habit of playing cards with himself in the living room. He displayed the pack of cards on the table according to certain rules and watched how they matched up. Björg had a habit of standing in the kitchen, stirring in a large pot. There was always soup in this pot.

I was their most frequent guest. Sometimes I contemplated cards with Magnús, and sometimes I hung about in the kitchen with Björg. On Sundays Björg always put on her Icelandic costume. She appeared in a black skirt, an elaborately embroidered white apron, a white blouse with large loose sleeves, and a tight vest ornately fitted with gold chains in the front. On top of this she bore a black cap, laid flat on her round head, with a tassel hanging down the side next to her braid. Her braids were turned up in the back and tied to the top of her head, under the cap.

In this attire she solemnly sat down in the living room, turned on the radio and listened to the broadcast of the Bishop's Sunday sermon.

148

If this is a detective story, the sleuth has been kept in the dark. The detective is not showing the cards.

Crimes can be hard to solve. Especially when the crime has not been determined in the first place. There is only a suggestion that something is wrong, but the sleuth is unsure which of the stories contains the clue. There must be one card, one piece, that can be used to tip things off.

The sleuth is worried that it is all a misunderstanding.

149

Perhaps the reference to the Hungarian boy is significant after all. He was a perfect boy, as boys go, except for one flaw. It was a speech defect. When he was to speak Hungarian, it was discovered that he could not roll his r's. There must have been some teasing about this, perhaps even yelling at him from across the street, in Budapest. Much later, when he found himself in North America and learned English, his defect came out as an elegant British accent.

North America, it occurred to me, turns out to be a place where major defects go undetected. Clues remain undiscovered. Former ugly ducklings turn out to be beautiful swans.

If there are scars they are all on the inside. Only occasionally do they surface, but when that happens it is a shattering experience.

150

In another version of the ugly duckling story, the duckling discovers that there are no swans.

The text admits that Hans Christian Andersen was a persistent man. He was a hopeful man, who may have spent his time opening clam shells. Somewhere in the longing, he must have felt, lay a certain extraordinary solution.

It was evident to me quite early in the game that it is necessary to make choices.

151

The writer gets a certain amusement out of rewriting old stories.

In yet another version of the ugly duckling story, there are swans, but there are two ugly ducklings. They are sisters, and when the swans appear there is a desire in the plot for the two ducklings to fly off with the swans. The younger one wants to go, but the older one stubbornly refuses.

It is not clear to the youngest duckling why the other wants to stay. All the ducks are gone, and when the swans have left there will be no one there. The younger one knows time is passing, the swans are beginning to take off one by one and it is necessary to make a decision. In the end the younger duckling flies off with the pack of swans, looking back often in a perturbed manner. The older one remains on the mound of earth and continues to get smaller.

152

The border between Iceland and Denmark is very visible. It is all water, and to cross over it becomes necessary to sail for ten days. In the beginning of the twentieth century, most of the food, the books and the medicine were still on the Danish side.

My father's parents died long before I was born. My grandmother, I was made to understand, was very beautiful. She became ill while still young, and the necessity of moving her to Copenhagen for medical care arose. But she did not make the crossing in time. Her illness made her blind, and after that she was not considered as beautiful.

At that time she was newly married to a young man who was also beautiful. When his wife became an invalid, whom it was necessary to escort along the streets, life took on a hopeless air to him. In his unhappiness my grandfather died. I was made to understand that sometimes unhappiness is a cause of death.

There was one child. My grandmother's blindness occurred just before my father's birth, and she never saw him.

153
This area of my father's life was never spoken of. It was never allowed to become a story.

All I had were indirect clues. After deliberating for a number of years, I sketched a vague trail through the woods. Perhaps I was thirteen or even fourteen. It is possible, I thought, that if the first face you see cannot see you back, then one of your daughters will refuse to eat.

In the metastory behind the story that was never told, there is a hint of politics. The text allows for certain backdrops. Often the text takes part in its own conspiracies.

154

I was left with the general impression that in the business of crossing borders timing is everything. If you do not cross the border at the right time, you run the risk of blindness. Sometimes you also run the risk of death.

155

On the last day of what I think of as my childhood, we were standing in line at Customs and Immigration in New York. We had an especially long wait since we were applying for immigration. Perhaps we waited several hours. During those tedious moments I was thinking of ways to refute psychoanalysis. My argument was that human psychology is determined by politics. And politics is determined by diet. That is, those who eat best win.

156

The text is determined to act like a demanding lover. The text demands of its author a ruthless honesty, which the author is unwilling to give. The author knows that once a quest for truth is begun it may possibly never end. Truth does not yield itself to its seeker. There is a suspicion that truth may not exist. Yet there is a certainty that what is being told is not a lie.

There is a further suspicion that if the truth were to appear it would be a paltry thing in rags. It would be small and bony, taking off its hand-me-down clothing and exposing its embarrassing skin. There would be a fear there, perhaps of a kind of leprosy, and an aura of hopelessness. It would be a speechless thing.

157

For the white Inuit children at that time, the lesson of patience was driven in like a nail into concrete. At school we were made to stand up and wait in silence until the teacher released us. In the summers we were placed in playgrounds in order to watch over small children. There we waited and watched for hours at a time. After school and during all school breaks, we were given knitting needles and wool. We knitted all through the evening, counting stitches and rows. It was a lesson we learned.

Perhaps for this reason the strongest memory I have of childhood is one of tedium. The slow clock ticking in the hall. The slow progress of wool being tied up into sweaters. The tired vigil over undersized vegetables that would never sprout out of the soil. The tedious arrangement of cans in boxes. The endless tiresomeness of watching small children sitting in sandboxes.

It was not a country where complaints were heard. We steeled ourselves. We clamped our mouths shut.

158

Pleasure, when snatched, was a stolen thing. Prowling was an act of truancy. The more you prowled, the more useless you became. It was possible to work your way down to the bottom of all public estimation simply by prowling.

I made myself guilty of this kind of truancy fairly regularly. For that reason I detected a sense of hopelessness concerning me. A resignation that there was not much potential in me.

For all that, I knew I had learned patience. I was the most patient of all. I could wait for months and even years. All it required was a suitable mental framework. A certain meditative stance. I had the business of waiting down to a science.

159

For some reason there were not many children's books. I had the notion that we were expected to read the books read by adults. Those books abounded. In the loft, where I had my dollhouse and my two rubber CARE dolls, there were numerous boxes filled to the brim with all manner of books. Paperbacks, hardbound, cloth-covered volumes on religion, literature, psychology, philosophy. They came in all languages. English, Danish, German, Spanish. In the living room, shelves on shelves held hefty volumes on mathematics and science. They, too, came in all languages. English, Russian, German.

I waded through these boxes and shelves. Hour after hour was spent silently reading with a total lack of comprehension. I read entire volumes in German, Spanish, Italian, without understanding a single word. They were simply words, with auras of their own, and they presented endless configurations of what seemed to be a very limited alphabet. I discovered that if one read slowly enough there was a peculiar pleasure to be had from meaningless words.

160

Reading in a language I knew, on the other hand, was a different matter. The added dimension of meaning appeared. *Meaning* was not always evident and always potentially terrifying. An altogether curious world seemed to exist, about which I had ambivalent feelings.

There were two Danish volumes of something called *The Living World*. They presented spectacles of bulging snakes that devoured large animals whole, and black people with sleeping sickness, who had froth on their lips and were lying on the ground. These were the true stories.

Then there were the false stories that were also true. There was Strewelpeter, who refused to cut his fingernails until they grew so long he could be wrapped up in them. There was the boy who refused to eat, who became smaller and smaller until he turned into a pile of ashes on the floor and the maid swept him up. And grim tales of children who were lost in the woods and then stuffed into an oven. Meanwhile the birds ate the crumbs on their trail. And incredible tales of people who were supposed to be gods and were tied up at a river while poison continued to drip down on them. It was a great relief that the one to whom this happened had a faithful wife, who sat beside him with a bowl and caught the poison in it. When she momentarily emptied the bowl, a drop of poison fell on his head, and there was of course an earthquake.

161

Of all the false stories that were nonetheless true the worst one was a book called *Palli Was Alone in the World*. Palli was an average boy, perfect as boys go, who wore shorts and a cap. He woke up one morning, and there were no people. He went about town looking for them, but all buildings, streetcars and shops were emptied. He did what all children would like to do. He walked into the candy store and helped himself. At the bakery he took what he wanted. He even drove a streetcar, and no one was there to mind.

Then he found the candy had no taste, the cakes were not good and it was no fun after all to drive a streetcar. He loitered about, hands in his pockets, and discovered that he was quite alone. It was not a good feeling. A great gap appeared in the region of the chest. There was sorrow, regret and a sense of hopelessness.

There was another book like it, which was stranger and even worse. There a little prince with curly yellow hair had an entire planet to himself. And another book written by, I was told, a relative of mine. There a princess, also with yellow hair, whose name was Dimmalimm, had only swans to play with. One day she discovered that her favorite swan was dead. Then she had no swans at all. It was her good fortune that the swan came back in the guise of a young prince, also with yellow hair.

162

There is a tacit acknowledgment in writing that stories that are true and stories that are false mirror each other. That in the business of stories, it is impossible to lie.

Those tales were terrifying because I had the sense that they were all, in their own way, coming true. They were prophetic, and prophetic in an awful way, I thought. None of the voices of reason, usually those belonging to my parents, were able to comfort me with the thin tinsely claim that the stories were not real. All stories were real.

163

Much later in life I seem to have been coming down the stairs of a large North American university building. A kind of gingerbread house in its own right. It had been a long walk. I was tired, and there was a vague sense that I had lost something. When I got to the bottom of the stairs, I saw to my surprise a face I recognized.

Some people have to wait for a long time for stories to come together. For pieces to fit. And there is always a chance, I thought just then, that the entire picture will slide off and shatter before the final pieces are in.

That face belonged to the Hungarian boy much later in life. The surprise was that a rumour had been suggested to me. According to the rumour something had happened along the way, and he was dead. But he was not. Just worn out for a time. It had not been a smooth journey, apparently. A kind of rough seas.

164

The text conspires in a form of truancy. There are derisive comments between the lines. A sense in the air that there is not much potential in the claims it makes. The text answers back: there are no claims. There is nothing to be fulfilled. Therefore it has nothing to have potential for.

There is an admission that duties have been shirked. That the text has been prowling in the reader's domain. Telling itself and then interpreting itself. Incorporating that which does not belong to a story. Posing itself as a question: it may not be a story. Perhaps it is an essay. Or a poem.

The text is relieved that there are no borders in these matters.

165

We did not have much to say to each other just then. I cannot deny that. It was a hot day. There were birds in every tree. I was wondering at how all images can suddenly crowd into the mind at once. All memories come tumbling down, scattering at random over the tilting floor. Cardhouses collapse. The Bishop recites his sermon on the radio, and seagulls yap about the ship, looking for slop from the kitchen. All things happen at once.

Behind this, I was thinking in a half-comprehending way, there were somehow guns, perhaps rockets. Fighter bombers flew across the sky, submarines floated in the sea, a couple of low-calibre bombs went off. It must have been in some magical country rather far away.

166

It must be possible after all to find a beginning to any story. Even if it is arbitrary. I have been thinking that there is an actual beginning to this story and that a story should end with its origins. It is necessary to conceive of time running backwards.

There was a first vessel before all the others that sailed between Copenhagen and Reykjavík. A kind of Noah's Ark of Iceland. Not the longship that journeyed from Norway in 874, full of small-time kings and chieftains looking for an island to settle on. This was the second Ark, after the war.

This ship was named Esja. It was 1945. All of the bright young men of the island were studying in Copenhagen when the war broke out. There was no communication with Iceland during the occupation of Denmark. The young people waited, and the Esja was the first sailing home. The students boarded with their new wives, their small infants, young children. Many of the young women were pregnant. They crowded into the cabins on board, and the men slept in the hold below.

The seas around Scandinavia were thick with mines that threatened to go off at any moment. The ship sailed slowly, hoping against all odds to miss the mines. It was a tense journey. The crew and passengers huddled on deck, in the cabins, in the ship's lounge counting their last minutes.

167

The captain of the Esja had never felt his responsibility so heavily before. He was later to say in public: we were carrying home the cream of our people. These were the educated ones, those who would have to build the nation and take it into the twentieth century. I had on board the future of Iceland, and one mine could shatter that future to pieces.

My parents were on that ship. They had told me that when the blue mountains of Iceland slowly rose out of the sea, on the horizon, the jubilation was unforgettable. Champagne bottles were uncorked, there was laughter, dancing on the wobbly deck. Now they knew for certain they were safe. And when the Esja docked in Reykjavík harbour, all the people of the island were there to greet them, with hands waving and voices shouting.